Masterson Murders

BY PETER ABBOT

NOVELS AND NOVELLAS
Librarian
Gukurahundi: Voice of the Lord
Hamiltonians
Quintet: A Novel of COVID-19
Armistice: A Love Story
Plague Year
Duty
Masterson Murders
Exeunt

SHORT STORIES
Gaiety

Masterson Murders

Peter Abbot

Rock's Mills Press
Rock's Mills, Ontario • Oakville, Ontario
2023

Published by
Rock's Mills Press
www.rocksmillspress.com

This is a work of fiction. Any resemblance to actual places, events, or persons, living or dead, is entirely coincidental.

Chapter One

Grey. That was Eric's first impression of Masterson University.

The buildings were grey, grey. "1960s Brutalism" he thought, as the taxi delivered him to the Main Entrance. He had asked to be dropped off there, so he could form a general impression of the Campus, before walking to the Library with his backpack and small suitcase.

Being well-organised and well-prepared were characteristics on which he prided himself; and he had carefully studied the small map of the Campus that the Registrar's Office had sent him, together with a letter giving details about the Interview he would be undergoing on the morrow.

In the Library, he approached the Inquiries Desk (which was ornamented with a notice reading "Just Ask Us"). Several students were chatting quietly as they sat nearby, on fake-leather-covered (yes, grey!) seats.

Behind the Desk, a bearded middle-aged man looked up from a book he was reading. Thin grey hair. And a displeased expression. "Can I help you?" in a tone that added silently "I hope not".

"Thank you. Could you direct me to the Librarian's Office?"

"I believe she's at a meeting. Did you make an appointment?"

"Yes, and I believe I'm a few minutes late. She's expecting me. She said just to ask you for directions to her Office."

"Ask *me*?"

"Well, whoever is on duty at the Inquiries Desk I expect she meant."

* * * * *

A few minutes later, he knocked at the Librarian's door.

"Come in." A warm welcoming voice, and when he followed her instruction, a young woman was smiling at him from behind a big oak desk. He closed the door and approached her.

"Oh, I know who you are, you're Eric, and you're almost exactly on time for your interview with Mary – the Librarian. About that Assistant Librarian position. She hasn't had a moment's break recently, and I know how pleased she will be to have really solid administrative support.

"Please sit down; I'm sure she'll be back very soon, she told me she'll slip out of that meeting as soon as possible. That Excess Pension Distribution issue isn't really one that's directly her concern, she said, even though there's such a fuss about it all round the University. But she did tell them her opinion about it at the last meeting.

"Oh – Would you like a coffee? I've been gabbing so much when – I guess you're thirsty after spending so much of the day travelling? From Halifax. I'm from Nova Scotia too, it's a long way from there to here in Southern Ontario, even if you fly, isn't it? Do you take sugar?"

Well, she *was* quite chatty – but that was welcome after his journey and the dour Library Inquiries reception. So they were quickly on first-name terms. Elspeth, "a good Scottish name, my grandmother was called Elspeth", and she told him that she was married and three-months pregnant with her first child, and that her husband was called Andy.

Then the door was flung open and a middle-aged woman rushed up to him. "Mr Merton – Eric – I'm Mary. Sorry to have kept you waiting – oh, these dreadful meetings when everyone, *almost* everyone, has to say what they have to say at least *twice* and as incoherently as possible! Anyway, there was actually a decision this time, *at last*. But I won't go on about it, you'll hear plenty if you come to us, in fact you'll be fortunate to hear anything else, ask Elspeth, we're all heartily sick of it. But you'll be really glad about the decision, Elspeth, I know – and I guess you may be one of those who does well out of it. Of course we'll *all* do well out of it, they *say*. But I wonder. It would be unusual if some didn't do much better than others.

"And I shouldn't be gabbing like this. Please sit down again, Eric. Will you be able to join us for a drink in the Faculty Lounge? I hope so. Or do you need to first –? Good! So we'll walk across in a few minutes, you and I. Once I've made myself look human again. You can leave your suitcase and, what's that, a satchel, is that what it is? You can leave them both here, Elspeth will guard them with her life! Thank you, Elspeth."

So they strolled across to the Faculty Building, Mary giving Eric a potted history and anatomy of the Library *en route*, and greeting the colleagues and students they passed.

Of course he liked her immediately and strongly, not only because her hair was (dyed?) red, and not only because she let it slip (deliberately?) that she "really hoped" he would soon be working beside her. "I knew I'd like you" she said, "a fellow Nova Scotian, and Eric's one of my favourite names – not that names mean so very much, do they, but I have an uncle called Eric – and you also have such a very strong c.v., and practical experience, and that's important. But of course I'm not prejudiced, just chattering."

Standing at the Bar in the Faculty Lounge were two of Mary's senior colleagues: one an elderly Fine Arts Professor known across Canada, as well as being internationally admired (Hugh), wearing a shabby jacket and open-necked red-and-green checked shirt; the other (Brandon) a History Professor and Mary's 'Adviser-in-Command' (as she introduced him), a thin hard-faced grey-suited man with (it soon emerged) very aggressive right-wing opinions on many (especially local political) issues – he was bald and clean-shaven (whereas Hugh was hirsute, with long white hair), and one of those men who uses his introductory handshake to signal power and dominance.

Eric was careful not to indulge his rather more left-wing views; at least he started that way but, being merely a visitor (as Brandon kept on telling him), found himself, despite Mary's subtle warnings, growing increasingly loud and confused – not helped by the generally rising noise-level as the Faculty Lounge filled. (It was Friday evening, a conventional time for Academic relaxation, as Eric recalled, from his years of Graduate endeavour. And it was near the end of term, with Summer close.)

Mary finally rescued him by rising and saying cheerily "Now it'll soon be time for Dinner, I thought Eric and I might go to a very nice little local restaurant – so thank you, guys, good to see you" and, as she and Eric walked over to her Office, "We'll collect your suitcase and knapsack, and then Elspeth said she'll take you to the Hotel we booked you into, it's not far from the Campus, and I'll pick you up later for Dinner, and you'll be able to have Breakfast in the Hotel tomorrow morning and then walk over to meet me in my Office before the Interview, which, as I think you know, is at ten o'clock."

Chapter Two

After a substantial meal, and stimulating conversation with Mary and her teen-age step-daughter Deirdre (who drove him to the hotel later), Eric slept quite well. At twenty-seven, he still had a good appetite, sharp observation, dependable memory, firmly liberal opinions, and a clear conscience.

But during the night he had an unsettling dream (as usual, before an important and potentially demanding occasion). And, as so often, it was about his Father and his Father's embarrassed apprehensive anger after Eric had happened, at the age of thirteen, to find him in bed with a prostitute, while his Mother was ill in hospital. A familiar dream. Or nightmare. But no longer frightening. A mainly-distant shadow.

So, the Interview.

The Interviewers included both Hugh and Brandon. (Was their presence with him last night strictly correct? Eric had wondered that afterwards.)

Hugh produced a meandering, evasive and barely relevant query, wondering how Eric would transmute his detailed university-level critique of pedagogic librarianship principles into increased provision of library resources for students of the Fine Arts. Brandon, as Eric expected, demanded a socialist interpretation of core Library values, and assailed Canadian Education for its signal failure to consider the importance of well-established paradigms. Neither of them focused on Libraries and Librarianship in practical terms; but were clearly the Big Guns for whose assault Mary had no doubt been preparing him last night, he thought. Her own questions were undemanding, almost apologetic. But practical.

And that was that. Eric was told by the Chairman to leave the room, "Just for a few minutes, I'll call you back".

The University Vice-President had been silently present throughout, as statutory member of the Hiring Committee; reading what may have been a Report, and occasionally raising his eyes to study Eric briefly, then smiling coldly when Eric looked his way. He left silently, as soon as the Chairman had ended the occasion by summoning Eric to announce his Appointment, on probation, as Assistant Librarian of Masterson University; which Appointment to be imminently and (it seemed) almost-automatically ratified by the Senate, as Mary told him later.

Handshakes, smiles, congratulations. "Now that wasn't too bad, was it?" Mary asked afterwards. "I know you have to go home to say goodbye to your family, and pack a trunk of worldly possessions. And of course enjoy some academic-year-end parties no doubt. Meanwhile we'll find appropriate accommodation for you near the University. I know that Elspeth has some ideas and contacts. But we'll talk more about all of that before you leave tomorrow. And of course we must also discuss which actual Librarianship course you'll be teaching, so you can prepare. And your library duties.

"Tonight – well, Elspeth has already invited you to Dinner, hasn't she, and before that you can spend time familiarizing yourself with the Library. I've remembered that I must accompany my Husband to the Annual Dinner of the Board of Hospital Volunteers, an important formal event – he's a business-man, and helps them with Aquisitions. So I must leave you now to get ready, Eric. But he asked me to say he's looking forward to meeting you after you return at the beginning of July. When you'll have lots of time, during Summer School, to familiarize yourself fully with the Library and University, while doing some lecturing, and working occasionally at the Main Desk, before the new University Year begins. Sorry to be so pedantic, but

I'm responsible for your integration into the University Community. Making you at home with us" and she smiled.

Elspeth not only had two possible rentals for Eric to consider, she and her very pleasant husband were a fount of information about the history and present state of the town and its rural surroundings. As they walked past Eric's choice (the cheaper rental, but his prospective Landlady, Elspeth had told him, was the widow of a retired Faculty member), "We love it here, we'd never move," she said. "It's a wonderful place to bring up a child. Andy's family have lived in the area for generations. Farmers originally – he still has relatives farming around here. And did I tell you he runs the local farmers' market, and owns the hardware store?"

"And what about *you*, and *your* family?" he asked.

"Oh, I wanted to be a doctor in Africa, like Dr Schweitzer, when I was at High School, but I'm quite content being a University Secretary now, especially in the Library. And volunteering in the hospital. Mary's husband is a wealthy well-known business-man, and also the Chairman of the hospital Management Committee, she probably told you. And I'm also very grateful to be happily married, and soon to be a mother, hopefully. I think I'm truly very privileged!"

And Eric considered *himself* privileged, too. He telephoned his parents that evening. His Mother was delighted that he wouldn't, as she had feared, have to move to Toronto, "that Big crime-ridden City", or, worse, to the West, ("so very far away"), for academic employment; and his Father, though he still looked at Eric warily, said "Congratulations, Son. You deserve it, after all your hard work. And sounds as if you'll be in a good part of the country, that's where my family came from, in times past, as I've told you – rural Ontario. But they were tobacco-farmers, wouldn't ever have been into a library, wouldn't even have known what a library is maybe. Now you can make up for their ignorance."

Back home, Eric called his three closest University friends and his girlfriend Emma, and was soon busy socializing. He had written his final exams, and undergone an oral exam, shortly before flying from Nova Scotia to Ontario for the Interview, and now the University Year was almost over. The two weeks back home would pass quickly, as his Mother observed while checking his clothes ("Probably for the last time, dear, so no complaints, we want you to look your best when you're with the other Professors and Librarians – you could get away with being sloppy, as a graduate student living at home, here, but now, as the Assistant Librarian in a bigger and more important University, you'll need to look smart").

Then, the evening before his flight, a shock. His Father, who watched the CBC Evening News regularly, said casually, when Eric came to say Good-night, "Oh, by the way, there was something about your University in Ontario – a death that may even have been murder, the Police say, it happened last night – some secretary, a young woman, I think."

"Who?"

"Didn't give a name, I think. But I wasn't really listening."

"Can I call them? It may –"

"Can't you wait till you get there tomorrow?"

Next afternoon he was delivered by taxi to the elderly house where he would be renting the attic apartment; and he was welcomed at the front-door by his Landlady, Mrs Arthur, widow of a History Professor (they had exchanged emails, after a brief telephone conversation, and he had told his Mother "she seems very friendly"). Her seventeen-year-old grandson Marcus, who happened to be visiting his grandmother, helped Eric transport his luggage up the two flights of stairs.

Then, after washing his face and combing his hair ("Too long" his Father had once said, "What's wrong with your Generation?"), he went downstairs and told Mrs Arthur that he should go immediately across to the University Library so they would know he had arrived: Summer School was to start in a few days. Also –

"Oh" she said. "But the Library will be closed by now, Summer Hours. And that poor young woman – she was a Secretary in the Library. The Police haven't got a clue who did it. They've even admitted that. We're all upset and worried, they even told us not to go out alone at night. But I think they should also have closed the University Library. That's where it happened."

"I'll need to go there tomorrow morning, to see the Librarian about my duties and so on. Was it –? How *did* it happen?"

"Nobody heard a thing. Nobody knew, apparently, until a Cleaner found the body in the morning. There's even been talk that the whole University may have to be closed – just when the Summer School is supposed to begin so soon."

Eric wanted to ask "Whose body?" But a huge reluctance was constricting his throat. And – Really, he knew. He knew that he knew.

"She was such a lovely young woman, everybody liked her," Mrs Arthur continued. "And she was pregnant."

Chapter Three

"Why don't you *telephone* the Library?" Mrs Arthur asked. "They always seem to know everything that's happening on the Campus. The Spy Centre, Jay used to call it. Jay was my husband, he was a History Professor, he always told me what was happening. Some of them still remember him."

"Oh, yes, thank you. I'll call them later. Sorry, I'm just useless at the moment. It's a big shock, I knew her, she was very kind to me when I came for my Interview last month. But I guess – I also should let them know, the Librarian, the Library Staff, that I'm here. Maybe they've cancelled Summer School – or the Library courses at least – but – I could leave a message."

"Now I'm just realizing that she must have been the one who called me about the room for you, I remember thinking what a very nice person she sounded – so unassuming, and she mentioned, I can't think how we got onto that, she said she was expecting – her first child, I think she said. If you want to call the University Library to leave a message – well, just use the phone now, or whenever you want to, local calls cost nothing as you must know."

Nobody answered his call, but a recorded message referred Eric to the main Masterson extension for information, and from that number he learned that the Library was indeed temporarily closed. He felt reluctant to call Mary at her home, and instead called Hugh, the Artist.

"Oh, Eric the Notably Infinite, back to torment our defenceless undergraduates! But I know I shouldn't be joking, it's a horrible thing, I guess you're calling about that – I think Mary's away for a few days – at a Conference in Edmonton, did she say? Maybe she doesn't know yet. So what can I tell you? But *I* don't know much, I don't think anyone does, and the Police aren't saying much. All I know is that it happened at night, or in the late afternoon, apparently she had stayed a bit late to finish typing an article for Mary – *she'll* be very upset, I know, when she gets back. But they may have let her know by now. And that's all I can say other than grief and lamentation, everyone says she was such a lovely person – I remember *you* did – a great loss, which our community certainly can't afford. And no, I don't know when the funeral will take place. But I'll be at my usual evening post, later, in the Faculty Boozer, if you want to connect."

Brandon was there also, unfortunately. "No surprise, this country's a mess, full of bloody murderous right-wing assholes" was his first comment. Clearly he was already half-drunk. Eric didn't stay long, but learned that the funeral would probably be in two days.

And back in his domicile, he decided to telephone Elspeth's husband Andy, to give his condolences. Though wondering if that was appropriate.

"Thank you. For calling. And your sympathy. It's – what can one say – it was a terrible terrible shock. Still is. It'll take me a while – No, I can't really – Sorry. And, maybe you didn't know, she was pregnant with our first child. But – and that was a great evening – when you came for Dinner, I mean. We both enjoyed it. Sorry I can't – I can't – She obviously liked you –"

Eric slept badly, on a too-soft mattress, his mind in distress. He woke feeling that he'd dreamed but, as so often now, unable to remember anything.

After the robust breakfast Mrs Arthur provided him, he walked across, through the Park, to the University Library. At first nobody answered his knock; but then a frowning middle-aged man opened the door. "And you are?" he demanded.

Once acknowledged and admitted, Eric made his way to the Librarian's Office – and found it barred with yellow tape and occupied by a large Policeman, who was taking photographs.

"Stay back. Why are you here, who gave you permission to come inside this building?"

After Eric had explained himself, and presented his new official University identity-card, the Policeman – who was, he said, Inspector Iverson – came out into the passage.

"Well, looks as if your colleague apparently stayed here after work just a bit too long, two nights ago. Stabbed with a sharp implement. Which we have not yet located. You say you weren't anywhere in the locality? You may have to prove that, Sir. Do you think you have any information that may help us find the perpetrator? Did she, the deceased, did she ever say anything to you – anything at all – that could give us a lead?"

No, Eric didn't think so, but he'd try to remember whatever he could.

Later, when he was sitting in the main Reading Room trying to concentrate on some old Notes that might be useful for his expected forthcoming 'History and Evolution of Western Libraries' introductory lecture, Mary was suddenly at his shoulder. "Oh, Eric, oh, Eric" and she embraced him, then held him tight, as he clambered to his feet. "Let's find an empty office."

The funeral was well-attended, by Faculty and some of the Undergraduates registered in Summer School courses. The University President, a handsome bowed elderly man with a slight stammer, read a Tribute to Elspeth, then, after the University Chaplain had delivered a short homily, they all sang a hymn ("Abide with Me", clearly well-known to all the older people present) that her husband had said she loved as a girl. One of Andy's sisters stayed very close to him throughout the funeral, an arm round his heaving shoulders.

Afterwards, responding to the President's invitation, most of the mourners walked across to the Student Centre for a muted coffee and light refreshments.

Mary held Eric's arm and whispered "We won't stay long, I couldn't bear Brandon just at present, do you mind me holding onto you like this?" "Of course not," Eric whispered back to her.

But Brandon wasn't to be avoided. "Well, Mary, so you got back in time for the funerary rites. And did you have a good Conference? Your Office gained some prominence during your absence, did you see its portrait in yesterday's paper?"

Mary smiled ironically. "Funeral Games, Brandon? But Eric needs some fresh air, and so do I." They went past him, Mary smiling rather tremulously.

"Poor Elspeth deserved so much better" she said, and he realised that she was addressing Andy, over Eric's shoulder. "Dear Andy, please let me know if I can do anything to help, anything at all."

Chapter Four

Mary and Eric met the following morning. Not in her Office, of course, but in his – which, he'd been told earlier, by his ill-tempered colleague at the Main Desk, he'd be sharing with "the lame Librarian", whoever that was.

"I hope this will work for you" she said. "As you've seen, we're rather short of space, though the Administration promised, when I was appointed, that we'd be given more space, for offices as well as another lecture-room. Anyway – let's proceed, though of course I know you and I are still upset, such a terrible death, such a good kind person – and, I guess because I'm a woman, though of course long-past child-bearing, it seems so horrible to me that, as her husband said, she was expecting their first child. Poor Elspeth. And poor Andy, such a decent young man, what will become of *him*? But I must pull myself together, we have other things that we must talk about.

"Now. First and least important, I guess you're agreeable to helping in the Research section? When we were discussing Librarian Responsibilities, before and during your Interview, I believe I did remember to tell you that we get occasional Visiting Researchers – none just at present, but any day, possibly, and I must give you details so you know how to help them; it'll be mainly your responsibility, as I hope I warned you. Oh, I've just remembered, there *is* one arriving quite soon, if I remember correctly. He's coming for a few weeks in connection with, I believe, a biography of a relative – I'll give you all the background info I can, once I can get back into my Office and have access to my computer, so I can catch up with recent correspondence. Which reminds me – I reminded *him* that a Member of our Modern History Department, an Assistant Prof, who has published in that area, has been researching in the Archive for at least a year, with permission from the Family. Her name, if I remember correctly, is Margery Allison. I'll introduce you to her if she appears today – but maybe she'll be taking a break this Summer. I told her she *deserved* a break! After all her hard work reading a very difficult hand. A very pretty girl, I think – but intense.

"Then Item Number Two. We'll need to talk more about your course and other responsibilities, you and I. But let's proceed to the Faculty Dining-room and we can talk about all that while chewing our cud."

As they finished their lunch, Mary announced that she would not return to the Library "until I can inhabit my new, substitute Office, probably tomorrow afternoon – they've found a small room behind the Main Desk, apparently used mainly to store books while they're being processed, and it's being adapted for my use – they're installing my computer there. I told the President I couldn't bear to go back immediately into my – well, I'd see poor Elspeth all the time, wouldn't I?"

Eric strolled back to the Library. And found turmoil.

At first he couldn't grasp what was happening. Shouting and pushing were unusual, and certainly unacceptable, in any library. Yet, right beside the Information Desk, a tall elderly man in a dark pin-striped suit was pummelling a member of the Library staff, while loudly insisting "You have no right to stop me, I'm the Senior Descendant, he was my *Father*, and *I* didn't grant *you* permission, I did *not*, they know they should have asked *my permission* and *you* know they didn't. And the Librarian knows that too."

The Library assistant who had reluctantly allowed Eric into the Library at his first attempted entry now came quickly across to him and spoke hurriedly, in an undertone, "My apologies, Sir, they shouldn't really have been admitted at this time, but the gentleman says he is Sir Harold Wallace, the senior descendant of Earl Wallace, and he says that he notified us a while ago that he was coming. I'm sorry I didn't know yesterday that you are the new Assistant Librarian, everything has been so confused, what with –"

"Don't worry, Mr Best, I'll see to it" and Eric strode to the Information Desk. "Good afternoon, Sir Harold, I am Eric Merton, Assistant Librarian. The Librarian is currently indisposed, but expects to be back tomorrow morning. And the Library is temporarily closed at this time because of an unfortunate incident. So if your research is not in any way urgent, would you mind waiting until tomorrow?"

"Yes, I *would* mind. But apparently I have no choice. So you will please inform the Librarian that, as I confirmed in an email a few days ago, I and my Assistant" – he waved in the direction of a young woman standing silently nearby – "have arrived; that we will return here at 10 A.M. tomorrow morning; and that I hereby request an urgent interview with her. She can contact me at the Hotel Excelsior downtown, between nine and ten this evening, if she so desires. And now will you please telephone for a taxi."

After the two visitors had departed, Eric was introduced to the attractive young Assistant Professor of History, Margery Allison, who had quietly observed the fracas initiated by Sir Harold Wallace.

"Quite a show" she observed. "You may wonder why I am here, especially at this time. Well, I was actually urged by his daughter to confront him, or at least keep him under observation – and of course she warned me some weeks ago about his intention of coming. He clearly wants to destroy my research project. In fact, he has actually demanded that the Archive should be closed to me, and it seems that the Library may have acquiesced – though surely they know it would be totally unacceptable to exclude any *bona fide* Researcher. You can see, I'm sure, what I'm up against. He has, or did have, a high position in British society. But when I wrote him, some three years ago, to introduce myself and ask for permission to publish a critical edition of selected writings by his Father, there was no reply. So I approached other members of the Family, and received not only permission but encouragement – as well as hints that Sir Harold was not liked or trusted by any of them. But then he suddenly erupted a year ago and totally denied me permission to proceed with my research. When I informed the Family, they said I should just ignore him. With hints that his involvement with some undesirable young woman might be motivating him – he's long divorced, and estranged from even his two children. But now –

"Well, I'm sorry to have gone on about it – bad manners, when I haven't even introduced myself! And characteristically indiscreet, Mum would say. I'm Margery Allison, Assistant Professor of History, and I know *you* are the new Assistant Librarian."

They shook hands and Eric responded dutifully "Glad to meet *you*, Dr Allison." And less dutifully, "We should certainly talk further, and probably this evening, as Sir Harold Wallace will be upon us again tomorrow, at 10 A.M. sharp. When the Library will be undeniably Open. How about Dinner at the Faculty Club tonight – at 9 P.M. sharp? And you can explain how and why you have been allowed into the Library today. Is Mr Best perchance one of your admirers?"

"That would be – Yes, thank you – lovely!" she responded with a grin. "I'll look forward to that. But we'll split the cost – I never accept favours from strange men."

Next day, Eric made sure he was at the Library by nine, its usual time of opening.

It was a fine sunny day. "Morning, Sir" said Mr Best dutifully as he opened the main door for him. "A lovely morning! And a good forecast."

"Yes, lovely indeed! Will the Librarian be in?"

"This afternoon, Sir. When her replacement office will be ready. That Sir Harold Wallace has already called to say he and his Assistant will be here promptly at ten o'clock, expecting immediate access to the Wallace Archive."

"Right. Can you tell me what you know about it, and I'd also like to know why Dr Allison was apparently told that she can no longer work on any part of the Wallace Archive – and especially now, too, when she is close to completing a major edition of the Wallace prose-writings for contracted publication with a reputable academic publisher."

"Oh, I don't think any of the Staff know anything much about that. Only the Librarian. She's the only one who has had any connection with Sir Harold Wallace – she said in a meeting that it was essential for her, and only her, to be in charge of the Wallace Archive and any issues connected with it – that's what he had demanded, and there was a lot at stake for the Library – I think she meant financially as well as for our reputation."

"Oh. Thank you for the information, Mr Best. May I call you Bryan?"

"Of course, Sir. Is there anything else I should do? There's someone at the main door, I think, probably a graduate student, and I should explain to him or her that we're still closed for the rest of the week – though surely everyone knows that, and why."

Chapter Five

Eric spent the rest of the morning in continued preparation for the course that he would soon be teaching to some dozen undergraduates; and then, growing restless, he explored the Library further, finding on its fourth floor a small well-lighted reading-area that he decided to make his own. "My Retreat."

After that, he made his way across to the Student Restaurant for a satisfying light lunch of pizza and ice-cream.

As he finished the pizza, a student looked his way, then approached to ask "May I join you, Sir, if you're not expecting someone?" And he sat down, smiled and announced "I'm Ryan, I'm a History Undergraduate."

And Eric responded "Hi, I'm Eric, new here – just hired as Assistant Librarian."

He greatly enjoyed their conversation, which gave him some useful information about the Campus as well as insights into Masterson student-life.

When he had finished his ice-cream, he said as he rose to leave "I should get back, but great to meet you – why don't you look me up in the Library? Just ask for me at the Main Desk, they'll tell you how to find me."

When he reached the Main Desk, Bryan said "Madam Librarian was just asking for you; she said to tell you she's in what she calls her Cubbyhole – just behind here, as you know. And don't forget our walk in the Park this afternoon, I mean if you still want the exercise. Sir."

"Oh, Eric" Mary said, as she opened the door to his knock. "Come in, if you can squeeze past me and sit in that ancient chair, I hope it won't collapse. How is everything, how are you settling in? After such a terribly upsetting start. To say the least. And I've been hearing rumours about your encounter yesterday with the redoubtable Sir Harold Wallace, and the redoubtable Ms Allison, who I gather is still very much with us – Oh, you know what I mean, I'm prone as you already know, to putting my foot in it. And I talk too much, my Father always told me that.

"But it's good that you have met Sir Harold and know what we're facing. He spent an hour berating me this morning, then apparently proceeded, with his Assistant, to re-check our listing of the Papers of his distinguished Father. I had assured him that all the embargoed material is *still* under embargo, for another year, and is safely stored – which he loudly doubted and again demanded to see what I had just again told him that even *he* is not yet permitted to access. Even as Senior Descendant! You must be glad that you have no responsibility for that particular bowl of cherries – Oh, I'm dating myself horribly, Maurice Chevalier, *Gigi*, I think, and definitely before your time! Maybe even before mine. I'm talking too much again.

"And I'm becoming more of a bore every day, talk talk talk. Will you have a coffee? Oh, but I'm forgetting: at 2 P.M. we will be interviewed, you and me, in my actual Office, by the Police, who will thereafter vacate it, they informed me – thank the Lord. So – Do you have anything to say, or has my verbal flow stunned you into silence? My Mother used to say 'Did the jackdaw get your tongue?' Or was it a blackbird?"

"No, not really. I've been preparing for my rapidly-approaching course, and had a quick lunch in the Student Restaurant – food not too bad. And I met a very pleasant, helpful History undergraduate."

"Well, five minutes to go, so might as well be on the dot. Let's go."

Inspector Iverson opened the door to Mary's knock. "Right on time" he commented. "Come in and I'll introduce you to Chief Inspector

McAllister, who has joined me from Toronto to help us solve this dastardly murder."

"I think this is your chair and desk that I've been using, Ma'am," Chief Inspector McAllister said, rising to shake their hands. "Please reclaim it – I'll sit opposite you, and the other two can sit on the other two chairs. Now – this was a truly horrible crime, and our sympathy to you all – but so far no clues. We're counting on you to give us all the help you can. We've interviewed the husband and family-members, and the Library staff. You were left to last, Dr Alderson, because you were apparently out of town, or almost, when the murder was committed; and Mr Merton, or is it 'Professor Merton'? Or 'Dr Merton'? – we understand that you had met and talked with the victim quite recently but were far away in Nova Scotia when the attack occurred. But please let me know anything, anything at all, that could help us. Did the Victim express concern or fear at any time? And why was she alone in this Office after normal working-hours?"

Mary shook her head. "No, she never expressed fear to me, she was an excellent secretary, and always cheerful, and such a kind-hearted helpful young woman. It was a terrible shock that she, of all people, would be murdered. We are still finding it hard to accept, and I know that my colleague Dr Merton – well, he will of course speak for himself."

"Yes, she was extremely kind to me when I came here for my job-interview last month" Eric offered. "She went out of her way to be helpful – she was very kind and considerate. It's hard to imagine why *anyone* would kill her. And –"

"And the murderer is still out there – or even here in this Library" Inspector Iverson said forcefully. "We have warned everyone to remember that, and to be cautious, watchful, and to immediately contact the Police if you see or hear anything troubling, anything unusual. Thank you both for your attention and information."

Afterwards, with Mary back in her Office checking her emails, Eric decided, after a short conversation with Bryan about the rules regarding Reserved Books, to go for the walk with him in the University Park, as earlier agreed. He also felt some need for exercise – "and fresh air, it's so stuffy inside," he told himself.

But he had hardly entered Mary's Office before he heard her loud exclamation, "Oh, no. Oh, Eric, Eric – oh, it never rains but it pours" (a frequent expression, he immediately remembered, of his Mother's).

"Two pieces of information, neither of them welcome" she told him. "The first is that a Senate provisional decision has at last been reached about the Excess Pension issue – which you know nothing about, of course, but you *will*, it torments us all and will go on doing so – at least that's my prediction. The situation seemed earlier to be more positive, but I and several others tried to warn them that a fair resolution could still be very tendentious. The second issue, which will come to pass earlier, is directly relevant to us in the Library. You probably don't know – of course you don't know *yet* – but every few years, and sometimes earlier if so ordained, and urgent, there is an Investigation, or maybe one should say a detailed Examination of University Departments, by CUT, the Canadian Universities Taskforce, of the CAU, the Canadian Association of Universities – an Examination of achievements, of particular characteristics and functioning, *and* of course problems and failures. Followed by multiple urgent Recommendations for Improvement. Now I'll have to read all this CUT information thoroughly, and call a Library Staff meeting so we can all discuss it, and review the implications, and prepare for the coming Visitation. I didn't expect this, of course – it's certainly not our turn – and it will be very challenging at this moment – not only because of, you know – but also because of various changes in Library Staff and Administration, like a certain new Appointment.

"Well – sorry if I've disturbed your afternoon, Eric, but thanks for being there, or here, for me and letting me offload some of my misery – you're fortunate that, as a new Appointment, you won't be much involved in all the machinations to impress our Visitors – but of course they'll want to meet and talk to you, as you are our newly-appointed Assistant Librarian. So – Anyway, don't let me keep you any longer from that walk in the Park. Enjoy – as they say. While you have time, *I* add."

Chapter Six

Eric returned to his lodging thoughtful but not troubled. He knew that Academia was prone to obsessively probing its values, processes and achievements: 'healthy self-criticism', it was called.

Mrs Arthur knocked softly at his door in the early evening. "Eric – you don't mind me calling you by your Christian name, do you? I hope I'm not disturbing you. But would you like to join me for a wee cuppa – as my Mother used to call it?"

"Oh no, of course I don't mind at all. I mean – That's very kind. And you're not disturbing me. And a wee cuppa is very tempting. Thank you."

They sat outside, on the patio, in the late sunlight.

After some light conversation – Yes, his room was very comfortable; no, he couldn't think of improvements – she asked, first, if he played chess; Yes, he said; Good, she replied – and so maybe, second, he might like to join her for Supper when he had the time ("But don't please expect a feast, I'm just an ordinary cook") and then they could play a game of Chess before bedtime? "I'm not a great player, as you'll quickly find out, but I love it, my Father taught me when I was a girl. I hope I won't disappoint you, especially now I'm getting old and feeble. My grandson Marcus thinks I'm gaga, I think."

He wondered if agreeing to her suggestion could lead to difficulties, but decided to chance that. She shouldn't expect high-standard chess from him, he warned her, in self-defence – but yes, he *did* enjoy the occasional chess-game.

And then she asked, casually, "Is there any news about the murder, do the Police at least have a suspect? Surely they must realise that many elderly people in the community, especially those living alone, are now living in fear?"

He promised that he would let her know any relevant significant news, and added that many in the University community were also very troubled.

At the Library next morning, in his small office, he struggled to concentrate while reviewing his notes on "Libraries and late-eighteenth-century English society". How important were libraries to Jane Austen? Did she use them? Could *Pride and Prejudice* have been written in the absence of libraries? Yes, surely –

But suddenly Mary was at his side, proffering the print-out of an email. "Eric, look at this. They're actually on their way here, say they'll arrive at 2 P.M., will interview you and me later this afternoon, and I should please assemble all the Library Staff for a Meeting tomorrow morning. I nearly emailed back to say that's impossible, with such short notice, but of course, as you well know, Summer School starts this week, so I guess we'll have to put up with it – and one mustn't offend them. And at least we'll get it over! So I sent a message that we must all meet *today*, all the Library Staff, straight after lunch – Sorry I couldn't inform or consult you before doing that, but it's obviously an emergency, and I must get back to my computer now in case – It never rains -"

"But it floods the Universe. Tell me what I can do. I'll check with Mr Best that all the Staff know. I guess we'll meet in the main Lecture Room?"

Half-concealed anger among the Staff. Especially when it emerged that Sir Harold Wallace was suspected of provoking the Visitation. Apparently he had been observed watching preparations for it with a smug smile.

"I think he may think he's teaching us a lesson" Mary commented quietly to Eric. "Apparently he told the Vice-President that his extensive contribution to this Library – what did he mean? He certainly had nothing to do with our acquisition of his Father's Papers, he was just a child then – and as far as I know he has contributed nothing but aggressive demands for impossible access to the embargoed Papers. Oh, no more about that, we've got enough to worry about."

The Meeting began calmly, but there was a perceptible undertone of angry resentment. With so little warning, and when everyone was so upset after the murder of a colleague – Mary tried to calm the turbulence by saying that it appeared to be coincidence, or some misunderstanding; and added that she had just had a telephone-call from the President to say that he would be with them very soon, and in fact he was probably on his way "right now – And I'm sure he will have information for us" she added soothingly.

And indeed he did have. After thanking them all, and especially the Librarian and newly-appointed Assistant Librarian, for their co-operation at what he knew was a very difficult time for them all, he announced that the two CUT representatives had been delayed and would not in fact arrive until the next day. However, he was glad they were all in attendance because he had some important information. It was a very fortunate coincidence that their meeting was occurring so soon after the Senate's Summer Meeting.

At that point, Mary whispered to Eric "Where's Mr Best? Didn't he get my message? I hope –"

"Oh, if he doesn't appear – maybe he decided to guard the Main Door, or guard the Wallace Papers from attacks by Wicked Sir Harold – I'll look for him after the meeting and tell him what he missed. He mentioned to me earlier that he'd be going for a walk in the Park after lunch and would I like to accompany him? I think he's a very lonely person but essentially kind-hearted, and almost too respectful, and obsessed by the Library Regulations – but now that we understand each other better –"

"What I must inform you, and all University colleagues," the President was saying, "is that the Pension Fund dispute has been settled amicably, at last. Regarding, as I'm sure most of you will recall, the final disposal of Masterson's Excess Pension Fund, so as to bene-fit the entire University of course. A settlement much to the relief of I assume *all of us*. For too long that issue has been a cause of debate and conflict within our University. So now we should all rejoice in the fair and amicable settlement thar has now been achieved."

Eric walked slowly back through the Park to his lodging. Since the abortive meeting, he had been reading through some of his lec-ture-notes in the fourth-floor corner of the Library that he had pri-vately named "My Eyrie". It was certainly quieter and, he thought, pleasanter than his Office on the main floor.

Mrs Arthur was waiting for him. "You're early" she said."Is it right what I've just heard about Sir Harold Wallace?"

"Oh – that he's responsible for the CUT interrogation?"

"No, I haven't heard anything like that. But about his heart-attack, is that what it is? My neighbour Mrs Watson just told me he's been taken to the Hospital. Apparently he fell down when he was walking along the road near the Park, where the taxi picks him up, appar-ently. Luckily his Assistant was with him. Didn't you hear anything about it?"

"I've just come from a Library meeting and doing some work for my lectures next week. But – Oh, oh, I forgot about Bryan – Mr Best – I was going to look for him in the Park, he told me he was going for a walk and invited me to join him. I'll just go across and see if he's still there, I won't be long – it was a few hours ago, but he might be still waiting there for me, I guess – I *did* tell him I'd meet him –"

Bryan Best *was* still there – face-down, under a maple-tree, a short way from the main path. He had been stabbed in the back.

Chapter Seven

"Not another!" Inspector Iverson exclaimed. "So here we go again. No, sorry, I know it's not a joking matter. Not at all. Didn't I warn you all? Now we may have to get the Mounties onto it. Why was he wandering around in the Park on his own?"

"I'm sorry, Inspector. I know I'm partly to blame. I was supposed to meet him near that path in the Park, but – well, it was such a busy day, unexpectedly busy, here in the Library, and I guess I had so much on my mind – I just forgot and I'll always feel very guilty. I didn't know him very well, but he was friendly and responsible and helpful. An excellent member of the Library Staff."

"I want you not to talk about it, until I say. Keep the murderer in the dark as much as possible. And you two, watch your backs. Literally. No walking in the Park alone, no working after hours in the Library. Absolutely. And I will need another meeting with all Library personnel – Staff and Readers."

"Oh," Mary objected, "is that necessary? They all know about the situation by now. The word has spread fast, of course, about both murders. But what about Visitors, and the Students who don't come into the Library?"

"We'll be putting out a general warning on the CBC – radio *and* TV; and in the local newspaper. And word about this sort of thing always spreads fast. What is essential is to catch the murderer before he acts again."

"Or *she*?" Eric asked. "Could a woman have committed the murders? And is it possible that this second one is a copy-cat killing?"

"Impossible to say until we're closer to solving these crimes. Why we must be so cautious. I have sent a full account to Chief Inspector McAllister, who is busy with other crimes in the Big City but will soon be back here again, I believe. And may order further measures. Meanwhile, please tell everyone in this community to be very very cautious. Very cautious!"

Back in her Office, Mary commented "The President is extremely concerned, I know. Not just for the safety of all of us – Students, Faculty, Support-workers, Visitors – but also for the University's reputation."

"And Sir Harold Wallace: what's happened there?"

"Still in hospital, and likely to stay in hospital for a while. I almost added 'Thank goodness' but that would be mean. He certainly created enough turmoil with his objectionable behaviour. No doubt, if you're an English aristocrat – if that's what he is, he doesn't *behave* like one, or perhaps he does – you get to thinking you are beyond criticism. But his Father was the real thing: brave, generous, and exceptionally observant; the best sort of Victorian gentleman, and then some.

"And now I should get on with work. And by the way, MUF, our Faculty Organisation, is calling an open meeting tomorrow afternoon to discuss the final resolution of the Pension Fund issue. I guess that isn't a personal issue for *you*, since you're only just starting to earn a Pension, but you might find it interesting all the same. *I* have to be on the stage, alas, smiling and representing the Library. It's in the Great Hall. And of course there will be comments and information about the two murders, and strong warnings to everyone, which will be a good thing. The Police will be there. I made sure they were invited. But maybe you have more work to do on your already-no-doubt-brilliant lectures?"

"Oh, don't worry, I'll be there."

That evening, during their second Chess game, Mrs Arthur said "I don't want to pry, Eric – my Husband, Jay, he always accused me of prying – but what has been happening at the University? Another murder! And is Sir Harold Wallace recovered now, I guess he's still in hospital?"

"Yes, but they say he's busy recovering."

"So he can cause more problems in the Library? What a difficult man – these English aristocrats, they think they still rule the world. My husband and I differed on that subject, he was a Monarchist and I'm not and never never could be, I say they're just flesh-and-blood like the rest of us. Check!"

And a short while later, "*Checkmate!* Would you like another cup of tea? Do we have time for another quick game?"

"Please forgive me if I go off to bed now, Mrs Arthur, it's been another very sad and disturbing and tiring day. I'm finding it hard to –"

"Betty."

"Betty?"

"Yes, call me Betty. All my friends do."

"Betty. Thank you for the game. I'm sorry I was even worse tonight – as I was saying, I'm not managing to concentrate very well."

Next morning, after a restless night, Eric was not unhappy to find the day rainy. If only yesterday had been rainy, he thought, Bryan might still be alive.

The remnants of a dream – or nightmare? – were troubling him. But all he could recall was the image of a grimacing masked face. Possibly surrounded, he thought, by other masked faces. In fact everyone in the dream had been masked, he now recalled. What did that mean?

At the Library, there was palpable tension among the Staff; and even the few Readers seemed tense and unwontedly quiet, whispering occasionally to each other.

His computer contained a restrainedly troubled email from his parents. Was he all right? *Please* be careful! Even in Nova Scotia, people were talking about the murders. And it looked as if Masterson Library could be especially dangerous – *two* murders of Library Staff members! So *please* –

He was surprised to recognise the attractive young woman who had arrived in the company of Sir Harold Wallace. She was sitting, clearly tense, near Eric's Office.

"Oh, hi" he said. "Would you like to join me in a coffee?"

"Thank you. I need to talk to you, Sir."

"Oh – not Sir, I'm Eric Merton, the neophyte Assistant Librarian, trying hard to find my balance. I've seen you with Sir Harold Wallace, I hope he's doing well, recovering fast?"

"Yes, much better now, thank you. And he asked that I speak to you, on a difficult private matter."

"Well, if I can help – But the Librarian is probably in her Office, and she could –"

"No, it was *you* he said I should contact."

"All right, fire away, and if it's beyond my concern or competence, I'll tell you immediately. By the way, we haven't actually met, officially, and I don't even know your name?"

"Oh – Ingrid. Ingrid Halvorsen. Sir Harold's Private Secretary. And – forgive me if being too hasty, but Sir Harold is very anxious that you are being informed that someone has been investigating in the Embargo part of his Father's Papers. That Diary, he said."

"But I'm puzzled, Miss Halvorsen – Ingrid. If what you say is right – I'm too new here even to guess – Why is it so important? The Embargo is due to be lifted in a year's time, isn't it?"

"But that may be too late. Sir Harold says that."

"Too late for what? Well, I'll certainly tell the Librarian what you have said, and let you know her response tomorrow. Let's meet again then."

When, as they were having lunch together in the Student Restaurant, Eric informed Mary about the encounter, she looked hard at him.

"So you're even seducing Visitors' secretaries now with your manly demeanour, Mr Merton. You were quite right to tell her that the Embargo cannot be lifted before time. Earl Henry Wallace, Sir Harold's Father, as the Donor, was very firm in his stipulation, and the Library must always of course fully respect his wishes.

"When I first came to this Library, from Toronto, some can-it-be ten years ago, the Wallace Papers had been recently acquired and there was considerable interest in them. *I* was interested, but – well, life got in the way, time moved on. However, I did read his famous *Memoir of Travels in the Orient,* and also the two early diaries on which it was based. Very vivid, he was a fine observer and writer. But in his Preface he referred to a Secret Diary which could cause havoc, I think he said, if made publicly available too early – hence his insistence on the Embargo which has upset Researchers and also caused such dissension in the Wallace Family. Though I must admit that, so many years later, the Secret Diary is very unlikely to cause ructions. Is that a word you know, 'ructions'? I wonder what its derivation is, must remember to look it up in the *Oxford*.

"Well, now I think I've outlined all I know, dear Colleague. Can you ask Ms Halvorsen, have I got her name right? when you see her tomorrow morning, to come to my Office. And now I'd better get myself ready for the Pension Fund *imbroglio*. Well, at least we know *that* word started its journey in Italy. And should have stayed there. Should I wear lipstick, do you think – or will that mark me as a fellow-travelling crone? So many decisions! Thanks for the lunch, my turn next. And please forgive me, dear departed Bryan. I haven't forgotten you, so soon, but –"

" – life must go on."

That's no excuse, though. For a very heartless comment. I *will* try to remember you, Bryan. The funeral is next week.

Chapter Eight

The Pension Fund meeting was very well-attended, and, judging by the expressions of angry concern on many faces around him, Eric assumed that it was likely to become contentious. As the final meeting of the Academic Year, with research, travelling and holiday-making stretching ahead through the Summer for most of Academia, it was a strange amalgam of urgent last-chance conversation and arrangements, closure, farewell, intense emotion and optimistic anticipation.

The University Vice-President made what he clearly hoped would be a calming Introductory Address, partly reminiscent, fully optimistic.

We were living in a time of great sadness, especially with the recent, unexpected and utterly unmerited deaths of two Library colleagues. Our sympathy and respect were with their families and friends, and their colleagues in our internationally-respected Library. But we all know, don't we, that alas, life must go on. And especially in a University, where our responsibility for the achievements and well-being of succeeding generations is, and must always be, fundamental.

What had been decided, after long consideration and debate, in regard to the distribution of the Excess Pension Fund, was clearly beneficial for the whole University Community, as would become undeniably obvious to all very soon. He knew there were some Colleagues who had questioned the decision, and had even suspected possible malfeasance. That was deeply sad, deeply unfortunate, and deeply unworthy of the tradition of faithful trust that had always governed the actions of the Masterson Administration, ensuring that the benefit of all should always be fundamental. So he hoped that, in the fine tradition of the Masterson Administration, indeed of the whole Masterson Community, respect and good faith would prevail in today's final discussion of the matter.

But that hope was soon bashed into fragments. Colleagues rose, one after the other, to question and negatively-criticize not only the Plan but also the dishonest Process through which it had been achieved (according to the unproven claims of several Colleagues). Was it true that financial or other rewards had been distributed secretly by the Administration to the Plan's Originators and First Supporters? And was it true that those Colleagues who opposed the Plan on principle had been unfairly and dishonestly penalized by denial of promotion and even questionable evaluations of their academic achievements? And was it true that widows of Faculty members, some of whom were in dire financial hardship, had been illegitimately excluded from rightfully benefitting?

The noise level was rising and the debate falling into imminent confusion, when the Vice-President suddenly banged his gavel loudly and stood up, a sheet of paper trembling in his hand.

Gradually silence prevailed. He cleared his throat.

"I have just been informed by this message from the President's Office of a terrible event, an appalling disaster. Our dear friend and colleague Dr James Hilton of the History Department has – He was discovered in his Office, this morning, deceased. Deceased. It's hard to find words, please forgive me, please excuse me – he is a loyal and admired colleague who retired a few years ago, and also an old friend, and to many of you too – In his honour I declare this meeting closed immediately."

The Vice-President remained standing while his colleagues filed silently out of the room. Eric waited for Mary to come down from the stage, and held her arm as they joined the exodus.

Only after they had left the building did Mary whisper, tremulously, that James Hilton had been a good friend over many years, and had "helped me very greatly to settle in when I first joined the Masterson Faculty. I should have kept in better touch, especially after his wife died. And I think he intended to take early retirement this year."

Eric wasn't surprised to find Mrs Arthur waiting for him.

"Oh, Eric, how terrible – what's happening, what's happening? He was such a nice man, he visited my Husband often in hospital and was so kind to me after Jay died. I saw him just the other day in the drugstore, he was struggling to walk with a stick but still so cheerful and polite. And he had been a great traveller, in his youth especially – he would tell me all about his travels in the Far East when he was a young man. Oh, come, let's have some tea, I can't bear to even think about it – It's so dreadful, especially if what they're saying is the truth."

Next morning, a subdued sorrow seemed to have settled over the Campus. The Canadian flag was at half-mast, flopping disconsolately.

Eric went up to what he was now openly calling his 'Eyrie'. His course was to begin soon, and he had begun to feel nervous. But would the University cancel all classes in honour of Dr Hilton? Probably not, as that might disturb the whole Summer School schedule.

He had received an email from Brandon. "Nil desperandum we all have to go he wasn't the saint they say in fact he could be a bastard. I know a thing or two about his activities." And Hugh had telephoned during the afternoon and left a message: "Good luck for your first lecture, Dr Doodle. I'm sure it'll be impressive, like you. Just don't snuffle, talk *slowly*, and don't *dribble*."

Chapter Nine

"So this is where the great Expert on the Importance of Libraries in the History of the World prepares his eminent lectures!"

Eric started. "Oh – Ms Allison!"

"Don't worry, my Lord and Master. I won't disturb you for long in your Royal Retreat. But I thought I should warn you that I will be sitting in the front row, eyes wide and mouth agape, ballpoint at the ready to record your august opinion on the Influence of Libraries on the evolution of *Pride and Prejudice*."

"Oh – but, alas, Jane won't appear today. Maybe you could ask a penetrating Feminist question about her absence during the question-period?"

"Indeed. That will be a temptation." She smiled and turned away. "But I will not risk further disturbing your deep thoughts now. Good wishes, and I know it will be a great lecture."

"Wait – how about lunch afterwards in the Student Restaurant?"

Eric's lecture did go well, despite a tension in the room that was undoubtedly caused largely by spreading knowledge of James Hilton's murder.

About which some garish comments had begun to circulate.

"He *was* strangled," Margery told him. "That's absolutely true. And – this is cruel and horrible, like the murder itself: he had not only been tied into his office-chair but also his face had been covered with slashes of bright red lipstick. Bright red Lipstick! Weird! Where did that come from – who even *uses* lipstick now? But maybe *he* did

– students and I guess maybe colleagues thought he was quite weird in some ways. But you know – I really don't want to think or say any more about it. I knew him quite well in the old days, he was my main History Prof, did I tell you? And in fact he was the one who got me interested in Eastern history and customs; and he also suggested that I should do my M.A. thesis on Earl Henry Wallace and his travels in the Orient, through reading and analysis of the diaries – which of course couldn't include the notorious Secret Diary that Wallace had embargoed. The one that I can't wait to see, as you know. – Oh, another of my infamous volubilities! I guess you'll have decided that I never close my mouth. Except to disappoint black-flies and mosquitoes. Please pass the pepper."

As she stopped talking, Chief Inspector McAllister was suddenly beside them. With a companion wearing an RCMP uniform. Eric stood up, and shook hands with both men.

"Don't let us disturb you" Chief Inspector McAllister said. "I just want to introduce you to Andy here – Inspector Kraft. As you may guess, the RCMP is advising and collaborating with us now, in view of the latest, very serious crime of murder that of course you will both know about."

"Yes" Inspector Kraft added, "and I'm still getting up to speed. Can you both come to the Vice-President's Office in half-an-hour or so, to answer my questions, give me relevant information?"

"Yes, of course" Eric responded. "I'm essentially free for the rest of today – if I can just let the Library Main Desk know first?"

Mrs Arthur was waiting for him when he got back late that afternoon.

"Oh, Eric, what *horrible* news if everything I've been hearing is true. I knew Jimmy Hilton quite well, and his wife Barbara before she died about ten years ago, he was a very sweet man, he visited my husband in hospital regularly. He had a fund of wonderful stories about his experiences in the Far East, apparently he was even a spy in China, though I always thought he was probably exaggerating for our entertainment. Who could possibly think of killing him? He was always such a nice man, the students loved him. And now the things they seem to be saying about it, the way he was killed – just awful, awful, I refuse to think about it, is there no respect? Come, sit down, we'll have some tea. And *I* have something else to talk to *you* about, too! It never rains but it pours. And then the roses will bloom."

Sitting out on Mrs Arthur's patio, Eric felt he was beginning to relax. A full day indeed, he thought: my first lecture here, and all the turmoil over the murder of James Hilton, and then the interview with Inspector Kraft of the Royal Canadian Mounted Police – And now drinking Earl Grey tea with my solicitous and ever-generous landlady.

Who interrupted his drifting thoughts. "Now Eric, what I've been hearing about that Meeting you said you would be going to, such very good news. What a relief! It'll make such a difference to me! And to many others, retired Faculty, widows and widowers. At last a decision, after all the arguing and backbiting! And once that money comes pouring in, I surely won't have to inconvenience myself at all by having to accommodate troublesome young people like you who can't even play a decent game of chess! Bliss! Bliss indeed!"

"Yes – but I wasn't sure about all that because I'm not up to speed with it, and the meeting suddenly ended when the terrible news about Dr Hilton came. And anyway –"

"Well, the President – I know him quite well, I didn't mention that before – he thought I might be upset about this latest murder, and of an old friend too, of my husband Jay as well as me, he said – so he called me a few hours ago, that was very kind of him. And he also said, about what we of course have been discussing, you and me – he said that the Pension situation has at last been successfully resolved, thank goodness! And he asked about you, and how you were getting on with Sir Harold Wallace, who seems to be an old friend of his, and I remember he once told Jay that *he* had done some travelling in the Far East, which was where he met Earl Henry Wallace. He's such a nice friendly man, the President, not at all stuck-up like some of those Professors that I've met here over the years.

"More tea? I'm glad you like my Lady Grey. But I'm afraid we have only cheese-on-toast this evening, I've been too upset to do any real cooking. But we can have a good game of chess afterwards, that'll calm us both and your game is really improving now, don't you agree?"

In bed later, Eric found himself thinking about Margery Allison – and his girlfriend back home. Margery was certainly the livelier, and probably much more intelligent, but she talked so much – and yet, was that a bad thing? He enjoyed it – mostly. And Ingrid Whatsername was also very attractive. He fell asleep in the middle of trying to remember her surname.

Then he suddenly woke up again, with a start. Was there really danger still, as Inspector Kraft seemed to suggest? Or was that just being over-cautious? In a place like this, academic and so to a considerable extent separated from the rest of the world, surely any violence would just be minor and momentary, an anomaly? Then the University's life would resume its calm, steady, organised existence, free of worry, unpredictability, turbulence. Yes. He adjusted his pillow.

And slept deeply.

But he woke up, as he often did, with fragments of a dream in his memory. What had it been about? Then a few words returned. "Is this a dagger I see before me?" Oh, oh – and he recalled his high-school English class 'studying' *Macbeth*. And then other words came into his memory – "Tomorrow and tomorrow and tomorrow… And all our yesterdays… To the last syllable of recorded Time…" How many murders were there in *Macbeth*? More than three?

He shook his head. No more of that, no more, he said to himself, just get washed and dressed, eat your breakfast (Mrs Arthur often provided porridge – "My Mother loved it, she was Scottish, she ate it with salt, that's the only way, she used to say" – and then, inconsequentially, he imagined himself replying "*My* Mother said she has Scottish blood too, 'The skirl of bagpipes always makes me shiver', she would always say that" – but oh, oh – this is ridiculous – *blood will have blood* –)

"It's a *lovely* day, Eric! Another one!" Mrs Arthur was sitting comfortably at the table, smiling gently.

Chapter Ten

The Library's routine was still novel to him and Eric found he was enjoying it: answering questions from Undergraduates, some of whom would be taking his course, or thinking of doing so; checking the Reserved Books against his copy of the list that he had earlier provided to Acquisitions; chatting with Library Staff, getting to know them.

But at the back of his mind lurked questions about darker matters. He tried to prevent them troubling him, and after two hours took refuge in his Eyrie.

Where Margery found him. "I've been hearing some complimentary comments about your performance yesterday, Sir. And I hear that even the visiting CUT Investigators were impressed. Did you know they were there?"

"Well, yes – I guessed that the bored over-weight woman wearing a long black sarong, and the ancient trembling bald man beside her, might be actually listening – Oh, Margery, maybe *you* aren't troubled, but *I* am – I shouldn't really be up here in my Eyrie, but the Staff seemed to have everything under control – and now that we're Open again, the Readers seem so subdued, even silent, that I'd probably only spread worry and concern if I carried on nervously patrolling the Reading Rooms.

"And yet – Where do you think our Librarian is? I found an email message when I arrived this morning to say that I should take charge, she would be coming in quite late – but she didn't say why. And I guess – well, why *should* she say why? – it's her prerogative, isn't it?

she's in charge, mine but to do and die. But at this time – Would she be insulted if called her at home, do you think?"

"Yes, I think she probably would, she's a take-charge sort of person, isn't she – she's a *strong woman*! But she also knows that *you* can run this place just as efficiently as *she* does. And it's not term-time, with a whole lot of new first-year students needing direction. So, really, it's a compliment to you, that's the way I see it. And she can see what *I* see, my dear Sir – that you're well-organised, sensible, competent –"

"Oh, don't lay it on too thick, Dr Allison, or I'll wonder yet again if you're being sincere – it's hard not to suspect there are ulterior motives at play when a superior Academic Professor starts complimenting a mere Librarian –"

"'Ulterior motives'? Of course there are! Haven't you noticed the way I look at you, slyly Feministic but also subtly but deeply impressed by your Masculine take-charge demeanour?"

"Oh, stop it – enough! Let's go down and grab a coffee, and I guess it's almost lunchtime. Will you honour me with your fiercely-feminist mid-day company?"

"And I almost forgot why I'm here," Margery said, as she turned away, "why I'm pursuing you down the corridors of power. I came to say this: When the Academic Year begins in September, you will receive an invitation to address the Masterson History Department's Undergraduate Modern History Society, otherwise known as Dates and Fates – to address it, I say, on a topic related to your current wildly-popular series of Library Lectures. The fact that I am the newly-appointed Advisor of said Society is of no significance, of course. But it *is* significant for me to be able to flourish your grateful acceptance. So speak or forever –"

"I accept. Gratefully. Though horrified by your display of academic partisanship, otherwise known as Plain Dishonesty. But – Oh, Margery, aren't we tired of all this superficial badinage? Let's be serious! And let's eat!"

* * * * *

Late in the afternoon, Eric had an unexpected telephone-call. "Greetings, is that the exceptionally-gifted and admirably-voluble Assistant Librarian?"

Hugh. "Oh, hi!" Eric responded.

"On behalf of our mutual friend Brandon, and of course myself, I'm calling to invite you to a Congratulatory Drink in the Faculty Lounge tonight. No, don't say, don't even *think* of responding in the negative. I'll pick you up in my decaying vehicle at your place of rest, Mrs Arthur's residence – a truly lovely old lady, I've known her for many years, sort of, and her husband before he declined into retirement. So, what is your response? Or have I dumbfounded you with my claptrap?"

"No. Thanks very much, Hugh, and for the ride – or rides. I assume you'll deliver me home, drunk or not. About eight? I'll wait on the porch."

Hugh was on time. And as Eric climbed aboard, he said "You must know, or guess, even as a newcomer, how these incomprehensible murders have shocked and distressed us all at Masterson, especially in the History Department, and especially all those of us who knew Hilton. He wasn't universally popular, in fact you could say he had more than a few enemies, but that's nothing unusual in Academia, we're a nasty destructive super-competitive lot – But certainly nothing to suggest he would be murdered, and in such a brutal way. I think you'll probably notice, even as a newcomer to our little academic society, that everyone will be unusually quiet and probably only a few will be there tonight – only the basic bibulous fraternity, but maybe not singing their own praises for once. And here we are." He parked carefully. "Friend Brandon will be propping up the bar as usual – or maybe not."

Not. But only because he was slumped in an armchair, with what must have been his third or fourth whisky, who knows, on the table beside him. He looked up and waved a boozy welcome.

"Quiet tonight?" he offered as Eric and Hugh sat down with their beers, near him. "Everybody frightened of the local Executioner. Want to guess who'll be next? Off with their heads! I could suggest a few comrades who wouldn't be missed. But that shit Hilton? Easily replaced, I'd say – not many mourning his dramatic departure, *red lipstick*, I heard! – well that's original anyway. Come on, drink up. And what's with our revered Mary, I hear she's gone to ground or whatever they say, whatever that means."

"I guess we'll know soon enough. But let's not forget why we're here – or why *you're* here, Mr Assistant Librarian. Brandon and I drink liquor in your praise and in avid anticipation of a great bibliographical – no, I didn't say 'bibulous' – future. Cheers!"

"Yes, cheers! It was a great lecture, your lecture, Sir. We could hear it, we could even follow your tortuwhatever, *tortuous*, that's what I mean, your tortuous argument. We are very proud, exceptionally proud, that our votes did that, we like to be on a winning side, hey, Hugh old boy, am I right? My lamented Father always said – well, who the Hell cares what he said, Fathers are a bloody nuisance, I'm glad I'm not one, never will be one. I hated *my* one, he was a royal bastard. Yours too, hey? Hugh?"

"I guess so. *My* one – well, he just abandoned us, my Mother said. When I was four. Three children. I had two sisters. 'Good riddance' she said when I asked about him later, in my teens. 'Good riddance! I loved him once, but he turned out to be full of hate.' She had to work in a store. To feed us. I had ideas of trying to track him down, to torture and kill him – one of those adolescent revenge fantasies. I guess. But he died, of natural causes, some ten or eleven years ago. One of my sisters told me. And I was lucky to win a university scholarship. So that's two of us who hated our Fathers and survived. How about you, Eric?"

"Oh – mine wasn't so bad, in fact he had to work hard, as a boy, on a farm in Nova Scotia. He told us all about it. Often. And he tried to be a good husband and father. But I guess all boys rebel against their fathers – hopefully not killing them in the process, or themselves."

Chapter Eleven

"I am the Vice-President, as you may know. And now also the Interim President of this University until a new President is appointed. The President resigned yesterday, but that news will not yet be widely known. I believe that the Senate will circulate an official announcement and decide further action imminently." He coughed and cleared his throat.

"I was asked early this morning, by Inspector Kraft of the Royal Canadian Mounted Police, Chief Inspector McAllister and our own well-known and well-respected Inspector Iverson, to call this Meeting. So, Gentlemen?"

Inspector Kraft blew his nose, closed a file he had clearly been studying, and said "Yes. Chief Inspector McAllister, Inspector Iverson and I are glad you have all come."

But where is Mary? Eric was wondering. Still no sign of her. I hope she's all right. He nudged Margery, who was sitting beside him, but her attention was entirely on the three lawmen.

Inspector Kraft: "You must be wondering what we have to say. Why we have invited you to gather, here in the Library. And we do have much to inform you. The case, or cases, that have concerned us all are now very close to being resolved, we believe. The murders of Elspeth Munn, Bryan Best, and Retired-Professor James Hilton. And I must inform you that Miss Ingrid Halvorsen, Private Secretary of Sir Harold Wallace, is now being sought in our continuing effort to shed light on the murder of Professor Hilton.

"So, while we understand the concern about the three sudden

deaths within this University community, we do not believe it will be long before they are all fully solved and your lives can return to normal. But meanwhile, in response to concerns expressed to us, we urge caution, and that you contact the Police immediately about any apparent threat or untoward event. Thank you. Inspector Iverson?"

"Thank you, Inspector Kraft. In brief, the basic elements of this case, or cases, evolved some years ago, when the then-President apparently instructed the then-Librarian to provide him with a copy of the embargoed Wallace Diary. He had obviously been informed that it contained very sensitive and valuable material. Informed by whom? We must assume, though she denies it, by the Masterson Librarian, Mary Alderson, before she assumed that office. Inspector McAllister?"

Inspector Iverson looked towards his companion, who said after a pause, "Here we should be careful. Much was at stake and much could still be at stake – though that appears much less likely now. I will summarise what we know. Earl Henry Wallace, during his Oriental journeys, learned about what was claimed to be a miracle cure for Pandemics that had originated in Asia. He carefully noted down detailed information about the cure in his Diary, but once returned to his home in England, fell ill and died – though not before confiding his discovery to his young son Harold. Who was then too immature to act on the information, or even fully appreciate it, and of course could not and did not prevent your University acquiring his Papers, including the Secret Diary, together with related material. But son Harold did remember the story, which he unwisely told to acquaintances like your Librarian's husband, who, some of you may know, is the son of the President of a wealthy and successful mining Company with branches in the Far East. And by the way, we of course have interviewed his daughter, Deirdre, who has now confirmed that her Stepmother had been so late returning home on the evening that her Secretary, Elspeth Munn, was murdered, that her Father was nearly forced to attend an important Annual Dinner alone. I hope I make that situation clear. You see where this is leading? Inspector Kraft?"

"Thank you, Inspector McAllister. Well, of course I wasn't involved until recently. But I can confirm all that Inspector Iverson has told you respecting background to the first two murders. About the second one, the murder of Mr Best, you have told us, Dr Merton, that you regretted failing to meet him as arranged in the Park. But someone else did meet him, and of course we know who that was – the repeated murder method, if nothing else, clearly informs us: Mary Alderson. Mr Best obviously intended to tell *you*, Mr Merton, of his suspicions about the murder of his colleague Elspeth Munn, and also he may well have, say, seen Mary Alderson reading the embargoed Wallace Diary.

"When we interviewed her at some length yesterday, Mary Alderson would not admit to the two murders at first. In fact, she denied responsibility absolutely. And we had no conclusive evidence. There were no witnesses to either murder, and the knife or other weapon used to kill the two victims has not been found. But it was in her eyes: I could see, and I think she knew I could see, her undeniable culpability. So finally she confessed – confessed fully to having perpetrated the two murders. She is of course under arrest – in fact, at this very moment she is probably being transported to incarceration in Toronto, pending a trial for double murder.

"Why, you may ask – why did she do what she did? She refused to tell us. So we cannot know now, of course. Or at least until her trial. Her reasons for killing two library colleagues – at this time, we can only guess – but it is very likely that they included a guilty recognition that her long obsession with the notorious Wallace Secret Diary was no longer the secret she had preserved for so long. But why, why, why kill innocent others – when even she must have known that the Diary's contents were now of little or no significance? But the long obsession, the shame? How does that Biblical quotation go? 'The heart has its reasons'? Inspector Iverson?"

"Yes, thank you, Inspector Kraft, where are we? Near the end. Right. Then who murdered Retired Professor James Hilton? *Not* Mary Alderson, it wasn't at all her style, her means of disposal. So, who? Well, as soon as we learned that Ingrid Halvorsen had fled, we knew. And the ex-President of this University has now essentially confirmed her likely involvement, and probable responsibility. Apparently she had been a close family friend, through a connection with one of his relatives when both were students at a private boarding-school in British Columbia. Sir Harold Wallace, still languishing in hospital, may be able to add further relevant information when we are able to interview him. So. Any questions? We have given you a great deal of information to digest, I know. Which we are still digesting ourselves. But it is our responsibility to warn you all. And we may not yet have gotten to the heart of the matter. Which is what especially concerns –"

His iPhone buzzed. "Excuse me a moment, please," he said, "this may be urgent." And then, "Oh, oh – and the Step-daughter? And the Husband? Have they been informed?"

"Mary," Eric whispered tensely to Margery, taking her hand. "Mary. Oh, Mary."

Inspector Iverson sat in silence for a moment, after the call; and then "Sad news, I'm afraid. More sad news. It seems that the Masterson ex-Librarian, Mary Alderson, has committed suicide. Pills – She apparently had a hidden supply of lethal pills – her Husband and Step-daughter say they had no idea of that. And we understand that, when she was allowed, under Police supervision, to select and pack some clothes into a suitcase before being escorted from her home, she was later able to swallow some pills that she had secreted there. That in itself would appear to imply guilt.

"Well, I know it's time we ended this – you must all be tired and troubled, and wanting to think of other things. And go about your business. But maybe we should just get rapidly to the end – or rather, the beginning. The very beginning.

"In the Far East a century ago – and then also here, rather more recently. What was in the Embargoed Diary that made it so important? Well – a fortune. Maybe. You see, we haven't had a Pandemic in

North America and Europe for so long that the vast majority of us have no knowledge and fear of one. But a few people have been arguing – medical experts and others – that one is coming. Soon. And that it could be devastating. Killing populations, destroying economies. So – If there is a way of preventing Pandemics, or at least moderating and controlling them, anyone who provides that knowledge will undoubtedly make a huge fortune. And so Earl Henry Wallace is our man. A great adventurer. A man of knowledge and ability. And in his Diary, he had apparently recorded, fully and exactly, how to do it – how to create and disseminate a Cure for All Pandemics. Priceless! If our assumption is correct. But of course it could no doubt take a few years to achieve that miraculous preventative and cure – years of experiment, of manufacture and distribution, one assumes. Or maybe not, in conditions of urgency!

"I have spoken to Sir Harold Wallace about all of this, at some length – he has sufficiently recovered, by the way, and should be able to leave the hospital very soon. His doctor certainly thought he was sufficiently recovered for us to see and talk to him yesterday. Of course he is very excited. But, as we know, the Diary will not be legally open and available until the end of 2020, which of course is a year from now – and the legal and practical arrangements will no doubt be complex and immensely demanding. And *then* Earl Henry's information would need to be disseminated and evaluated by medical experts." He paused to clear his throat and blow his nose.

"Well, I guess that *is* enough for one day? You have all been patient and I have been garrulous. But we thought it important that the whole situation should be as clear as possible, and fully explained – justified. And now I should thank you all – Inspector Kraft and Inspector McAllister and I are grateful for your patience and understanding. And I'm sure we agree that just talking about these painful and dangerous matters with you all has been very helpful in clarifying what is not your regular clear simple murder-solution."

Chapter Twelve

"Poor Mary. I still think that. And I still think that she's not guilty. But maybe I shouldn't. She was clearly under a lot of pressure, and I didn't know, I didn't even notice. She seemed so totally in control, but – What's that poem, 'Not waving but drowning', she was *drowning* and I never even even noticed. Did anyone? She always seemed so confident, so –"

"She also murdered two close colleagues, Eric! And she could have murdered *you*."

"Oh, I don't think so. But to think she could even *think* of killing those two colleagues – that makes one shiver. And maybe I should have – well, maybe I missed clues. If I'm wrong and missed all the clues – if she really did do – what the Police say – Maybe she was actually appealing for help, and I was too stupid or self-absorbed to notice."

"You shouldn't blame yourself, Eric. She murdered two people, both of whom you liked and admired. Feel sorry for *them*! And for those who loved them. And remember, Bryan Best's funeral is still to come. Oh, Eric, let's dance, let's not talk any more about it – or think about it – And remind yourself that *you* could have been one of her victims."

"I told you I *can't! I truly can't* dance, Margery. I can't. No sense of rhythm, ask my Mother."

"Nonsense. We all got rhythm. Come on."

Sitting back on a bench, Eric gasped, "I'm so out of condition."

"Out of breath. Out of sorts. Out of money. Out of luck. Out of your mind." Margery sat down beside him.

"Oh, stop it, you heartless harridan!"

"Now, that's more like it! I admire a man with some guts, as long as they don't hang out too far – when they would be likely to keep his eager companion at bay. Well, change the topic, You! Once your breath returns."

"Right. Jane Austen. *Pride and Prejudice*. You Elizabeth. Me Darcy. Avaunt, Lady de Burgh – do I have her name correct? Discuss."

Margery giggled. "Stupid stuff, Herr Librarian. All right, how about this? *Tomorrow's Achievements Today!* or *Forward with Integrity!!!!* Have you encountered the latest Masterson Mottoes? We laughed and laughed, my little covey of weird witches. *Double, double, toil and trouble!*"

"Well, I've got my breath back, Lady de Lust. Shall we dance again? Or maybe not. But I fear the night is ageing fast."

"Only if you unscrew your left foot, the one that seeks out my delicate toes in order to squish them so painfully."

He stood. Then turned away from her. Mary, oh Mary. Mary. Am I betraying you? Are the Police right, do they know what they're doing?

Margery watched him, intuiting his pain and confusion.

Then he said "Margery – I need the washroom. But I'll be back. In a trice. Please wait for me."

"I'm so glad to meet you, Margery." Mrs Arthur smiled and held out her hand. "I hope you can join Eric and me for a cup of tea and a chat."

"Yes, of course. It's a great pleasure, I've heard so much about you and your great meals and conversation."

"And his superior ability as a chess-player, he does *try*, sometimes, but he's so easily distracted, and of course he's a man."

"Yes, I've noticed. I hope he's told you that we have just agreed to get married next summer, nobody gets engaged these days, and of course we very much hope that you will be –"

"– his Fairy Godmother, yes of course, I'm delighted and honoured, but he hasn't said a word yet, do you think he's fallen asleep?"

Eric grimaced. "Two women together, one young and ugly, the other old and even uglier, and desperately clutching her Pension Excess Reward – But all this Feminist nonsense – you said you had news for us."

"Yes, I do." Mrs Arthur carefully poured and handed them cups of steaming Lady Grey tea.

"That kind Inspector Iverson called, I like him, he's always so pleasant and respectful, and he said he had confidential information about the death of my old friend Jimmy Hilton. That he must have been killed, yes, by that Ingrid woman, he said, but also it's so much more complicated than we thought, he said. It was 'an act of revenge', the Inspector thinks. She had been a student of Jimmy Hilton's years ago, she took his course because she had been told he was an expert on Chinese history and had travelled in China when he was a young man, Inspector Iverson said. They had located one of her friends, who told them that the Ingrid woman had distant Chinese relatives, and she longed to visit China. But he had deceived her completely, she told her friend. And also she said Jimmy Hilton had abused her, it was after his wife died, and that he had in fact, I don't like to say it, she said he had raped her. But I don't believe that. I don't.

"There, that's about it, what the Inspector told me, and I know you won't tell anyone else – but I really can't believe it, he was such a nice man, Jimmy Hilton, and his wife was always a very good friend to me. There, that's it. I've said it, now – what Inspector Iverson told me in confidence, I know you won't tell anyone else – and now I want to forget it, how can people be so cruel to each other? *Please* help yourselves to some cookies, I made those yesterday for a Young Man who, let me warn you, Young Lady, doesn't eat nearly enough, which is why he's so painfully thin and plays such a bad game of chess. More tea?"

"Thank you, Mrs Arthur, they're lovely. But our great Librarian better not expect his little Wifey to bake him cookies – and he'll have to dance for his supper every night, and no reading of Jane Austen will be permitted – except in the Library, safely out of mischief, which is where she belongs."

Eric stirred. "And where *he* belongs, especially if his ears and brain are constantly afflicted by domestic tirades. Did I tell you I had a nightmare the other night, all about *Macbeth* and his knife?"

"Oh – *Mac the knife?* I've heard that one. But let's get real. Your landlady and your wife-to-be have just announced that we will in no way tolerate anything but the highest standards of behaviour from a University Librarian."

"Which I'm not."

"*Yet.* But Mrs Arthur and I will be taking imminent action to ensure that you *will* be, one day very soon. It's called Academic Politics."

"Oh. I'm speechless, as you can hear."

Chapter Thirteen

Mrs Arthur had been waiting for him. "Tiring day? Come and sit down and relax. I'll make us some Lady Grey. So it's back to normal? How did your lecture go?" over her shoulder as she headed for the kitchen.

"Oh, not too bad, they're a pleasant group of students – so far, anyway. They'll probably tear me apart once they've settled in." Eric was glad to sit in a comfortable chair.

"So it's back to normal?"

"Well – not exactly. I guess it'll take a while for the tension to go. In the main Reading Room especially, the students were exceptionally quiet when I patrolled – I guess they all know now about, you know, Mary."

Mrs Arthur sat down and poured their tea.

Then she said abruptly "I lost my temper this morning with one of my friends, she insisted on talking about – well, you know the Pension Excess Plan that is now apparently resolved. Some time ago, your Librarian wrote an open letter to the President, who has now resigned of course, and apparently there's some speculation about that. The letter questioned the procedures and allocations, and also asked why some widows of deceased Faculty members had been *completely excluded* from the Pension Plan – as I thought at one point I had been. But my friend, maybe now my *ex*-friend, said she had heard quite a few comments at the time, that the Librarian should be gotten rid of. Just for saying what she thought – So she wasn't surprised, my ex-friend said, to hear about 'violence in the Library'. – But that's all just water under the bridge now, even if it leaves a nasty taste in one's mouth. Sorry if I've upset you, telling you that. It's been on my mind. More tea? And you haven't touched the cookies."

"No, sorry. Not really hungry – but I will be, later. Can I have a rain-check?"

"And before I forget, there was a phone-call for you about half-an-hour before you came in. From, I think he said his name was Hugh – which was my favourite uncle's name, he taught me how to skate, and play hockey with the boys. He wanted you to call him – so, once you've finished your tea – And also don't forget, the doctor has ordered you to play a game of chess with your landlady before you go to bed tonight."

"Oh, there you are, Eric. Hugh here. Can you meet me in the Booze Barn tonight? Or I can pick you up in an hour or so – you've prob-ably just got in. Hope you've had a good day."

"Is it important?" Eric asked. "Must confess I'm quite exhausted."

"Well, we could go on talking like this if you like."

"Oh, no – If you could pick me up as you said, and return me in one piece by ten o'clock latest –"

"Will do. Please give my regards to Mrs Arthur, also tell her that when we spoke earlier I wasn't sure she remembered me. I hope she didn't think me abrupt."

Mrs Arthur: "Yes, of course I remember him, and yes, he *was* abrupt. Tell him he's unforgettable, alas. Oh, better leave out the 'alas'. So you'll be going to that den of iniquity again – even when no doubt you would claim to be *much* too exhausted to engage in a game of chess with your dear landlady. Oh, don't mind me, Eric," as she no-ticed his pained expression, "I'm just teasing you, of course. See how your presence enlivens this old lady!"

"Hi, Eric. You must be wondering what this is about. Just when everything seemed to be starting to settle down. Maybe. I won't keep you in the dark. It's about our friend Brandon. Who is – Well, I'll give you a full account when we meet up with a few of his very-concerned colleagues imminently. Then I won't have to repeat myself."

The colleagues, three of them, were drinking and chatting at a table near the bar, with two beers waiting for Eric and Hugh.

After introductions, Hugh said briskly, "I won't delay telling you that our mutual friend Brandon is in jail, and will spend the night there. He called me couple of hours ago. How it happened, he explained, was that he had called the Police Station about his suspicion that there was some scandal in that Excess Pension Fund disbursement, whatever it's called – he had told me about his suspicions a while ago, but now, he said, he had *evidence* –"

"Of what?"

"Said he'd tell me later. 'Walls have ears –' But the Police weren't interested anyway, or maybe they couldn't understand his slurred speech if he'd been drinking, as he probably had been – And anyway he confessed that he wasn't absolutely sure he was remembering correctly and maybe he should just – And they said he was too impaired to set off home and he should spend the night there, in the prison – he could sleep in a cell! But there's apparently some new and important development relating to the murder of James Hilton, and they seem to have actually suspected *Brandon*, can you believe it! That's what he seemed to be saying. He had been anonymously fingered, is that how you say it, *fingered* to them, as a suspect, a bit earlier, just after the murder – apparently he'd had a run-in with Hilton more than once. And had even been heard threatening to *kill* Hilton! Some heated disagreement over who started the First World War, apparently! Anyway, Brandon wanted me to give him an alibi for the night Hilton was murdered. But I couldn't – that was my euchre night. Every Thursday. So can any of you –? Eric, did *you* come here that night? I don't think so."

"No. I haven't been here for a while – too much else going on, for a start. Sorry. But surely it'll be all right? I can't imagine Brandon killing *anybody*, especially at night – he's almost always *here* then, isn't he? And –"

"Yes," said one of the colleagues "and always blind drunk. Might even be good for him to spend a night or two in jail, but don't tell him I said that. I have to say he's a bit of a drag in the Department. Sorry, I didn't mean to say it like that. I even heard the Dean was trying to find a way to get rid of him. Poor teaching-evaluations, et-cetera. Even some missed lectures. And no research projects. So this prison experience – well, could be beneficial for him, maybe? Shock him into changing his ways. Before it's too late. I always think he's missing his old life. Whatever that was?"

"Oh, we know what that was. Is. It'd be better for him to face up to the fact that he's gay, quite a few of us think that. Don't you agree?"

An hour later, Hugh drove Eric to Mrs Arthur's house, in silence. And the silence deepened after Hugh stopped the car at the entrance-gate.

Eric opened his door, but then sat unmoving, in silence, for a few moments. Then said "I'm troubled, Hugh, as you have no doubt noticed." He closed the door.

"About Brandon?"

"No, not so much – he'll be all right, won't he? When you pick him up tomorrow morning, please give him my good wishes. No – about Mary. Mary. And her suicide. I just can't – I just can't –"

"Eric – What can I say? Just that you've got a lot on your plate, and maybe it's not the time to talk or even think now about those things."

"That's what I've told myself, over and over, but – Why? Why? She was – I *know* she was – a good person. I can't believe – I just *can't believe* – Murder.* And *suicide* – And I thought it was long-established that women don't murder with *violence*, as men often do. Isn't that right?"

"Enough. Please, Eric. We both have worries, we both need to get some sleep. I'll call for you tomorrow morning at eight and we'll talk then. But now – no chess tonight! Tell that old harridan, if she's waiting up for you, tell her that you're already checkmated. Right? And *get some sleep.*"

Chapter Fourteen

"Oh, there you are, Eric. Now sit down and eat your porridge – my Mother, she was Scottish, always said nobody should start the day before eating his porridge – half the troubles of the world come from not starting the day with a good breakfast, she would say –"

"And the other half come from believing and constantly *saying* that. Oh, sorry – see what a bad influence you are on a well-brought-up young Maritimer – wait till you meet *my* Mother, I've been telling her about you and how you try and try, and fail, to influence my impeccably innocent and honourable behaviour with your immoral conversation and endless mindless chess-playing."

"Oh, get on with it. You have a nasty streak. And Hugh's waiting for you out on the deck. Actually, I quite like him, he said he can't play chess but I offered to teach him – and we had a good chat before you arrived, and he promised to come for tea very soon. So don't keep him waiting now, eat your breakfast! And what about Margery? You'll lose her if you don't show a bit more gumption."

A quick breakfast, then Eric hurried out to Hugh. "Sorry, I overslept, but is there anything important? I didn't expect you to pick me up and you'd better not let me get used to you giving me a ride to work!"

"Oh, I won't, don't worry, this is mainly because you worried me a bit with your Mary, Mary, Mary – we all just have to accept what happened, we're all old enough to know you can't change what's happened – and often people aren't what they seem to be. And remember that we live in the Age of Feminism and Strong Women."

"And what's that supposed to mean?"

"Oh, only that – oh, I don't know *what* I mean. I'm as confused and troubled as you are."

The phone rang just after Eric had reached the Library and sat down at what still seemed to him to be Mary's desk in Mary's office.

"Surprise, surprise!"

"Brandon? Is that you? Are you Out? At home?"

"Out and about. And about Out. And very sober. And in my new home."

"New home?"

"What's the matter with you this morning? Are you still waking up? Do I have to say everything three times? Listen up. Because I got news for you. *Are you listening now?* Hugh has proposed and I have accepted. We will get married in the Fall, and we are inviting you, yes *you*, to give us away, whichever one you wish to give to the other one, and then vice-versa. Are you following me or is it still too early for your pea-brain to function? Don't you have a class to give this morning? The future of Libraries and Librarians, here and everywhere, depends on you. Now get with it!"

"No, thank goodness. No class today. And I think I must be still asleep. I assume you're in Hugh's office, so please hand the telephone to him."

"Hugh here. So you see – Brandon wanted to break our big news to you. He will be the dominant partner who cooks and makes our bed every morning. That was my main condition. It all happened very suddenly a couple hours ago, before I picked you up, when I picked *him* up at the police-station. Don't ask me to explain any of it. Call it a Happening that finally Happened. In my ancient vehicle. I think it finally dawned on my Mate-to-be, during his cold vulnerability last night – during a sudden sense of discomfort and menace, within a lonely prison cell – that rescue was at hand – that Canada, like most of the Western World, had come at last to its senses, escaped at last from mental and moral isolation and incarceration, and welcomed Reality, the Reality of same-sex love and marriage. Yes, Brandon's shaking his head up and down – in agreement or admiration, who knows. Or both. My longest speech yet!

"And *you* know what *I'm* thinking, Eric, and *I* know what *you're* thinking. Actually – I know that she – Forgive me for weeping as I try to say it. Because she would have been – oh, Mary – Mary – There. I *have* got feelings. After all. And now *you* must get with running the Library, and *I* must – We'll see you tonight in the Faculty Beerhall and *celebrate!* All three of us. Right? We'll pick you up at eight, and please tell your Landlady she doesn't deserve it but she's invited too."

At the Library there was a feeling of uncertain normality. Undergraduates filed along passages beside stacks, looking for books on their course reading-lists; some of them smiled and nodded at him; others sat talking quietly with friends. In some of the reading-rooms, graduate students were scrutinising old documents. As Margery used to do, Eric thought – I must call her.

Yes, but – His mind still seethed with questions and concerns. The two Library murders had been solved – however painfully. But there was as yet no closure to the murder of James Hilton. Surely the Police couldn't really believe that Mary killed *him* too? And what were the Police doing?

Chapter Fifteen

When she got back that morning to her University Residence, after giving her first Summer School lecture, Margery was surprised, as she checked for emails, to find a message from Eric: "URGENT, call me NOW at my Office."

He answered the telephone immediately. "Oh, thank goodness. There's been – When I got back here an hour ago, totally breathless after a quick run to try to get rid of some of that hideous flab you have been objecting to, they told me the Police had been trying to contact me, and there was also a message from Mrs Arthur to that effect."

"But what's it all about? Sounds weird."

"Yes. But I think our friend Sir Harold is at the bottom of this. Apparently he has been in contact with that RCMP man, Kraft, demanding his intervention to secure 'immediate access' to his Father's infamous Secret Diary, and he seems to have made various wild accusations, with reference to speculated involvement in what he called 'skulduggery leading to violence and murder and probably damage to the Diary or even its loss'. I checked to be sure it's still with us, and of course it is, safely in its red box. As I immedately informed the Police. But they are still coming, and so is Sir Harold, this afternoon. Moreover, the Library must 'remain vigilant', I was instructed. Really, I think it's all meant to cause us maximum inconvenience, and give an opportunity for the Police to check on our safety and emergency protocols – and for Sir Harold to throw his weight around again before, hopefully, he departs for good. Or evil. So I must stay here, check our defences, and await our fate. The great meeting is scheduled for 2:30 P.M. – so could we meet here at say four-thirty, go for a walk and then have dinner? I guess I'll have to starve till then –"

"Oh, I'll bring you some sustenance."

"No, you will *not*. One of the Staff has offered to get me coffee and sandwiches. I was exaggerating, sorry."

"Well, let me not pre-empt your attention, Dr Assistant Librarian, Sir – just let me know what's happening, as soon as *you* know."

"Right. I love you."

"Oh, do you? That's the second or third time you've said that, so maybe we need to talk about it, before it becomes a habit."

"And that's the first time *you've* said *that* to *me*."

"Said what?"

Eric tried to occupy himself with tidying the Librarian's Office, glancing through some of Mary's most-recent email correspondence, none of it seeming at all unusual or suspicious; and, after that, beginning to familiarize himself with the Library Budget, Acquisitions, and so on.

Then there was a telephone call. "Is that Professor Eric Merton? Inspector Iverson here. Are you alone?"

"Yes. Can you please tell us what's happening?"

"With our apologies, McAllister's and mine. Seems that we jumped the gun, shouldn't have called that meeting and revealed so much, maybe – a lesson in caution for us – McAllister says we should be really embarrassed. Of course *he* blames *me*. Says I was irresponsible. And Kraft blames us *both* and threatens to have us disciplined. But that's not the main point, of course. The main point is that we know a murderer's still out there."

"But I thought –"

"Well, *we* thought too, that's what I'm saying. But now we know the young lady, Ingrid Halvorsen, has a perfect alibi: she spent that day and night with an old University friend, he's a Gerontology Lecturer now, at your University, and he went away for a few days to visit his parents in Ottawa, one of them's very sick, apparently – and the young woman went with him, and they just returned last night.

"So we're back to square one: Who murdered Professor James Hilton? The Campus Police, and of course our local Officers, have all been informed and alerted. We think it's unlikely that you in the Library, and of course we're concerned about Students as well as your Staff, but we think that you probably aren't in any danger. That murder seemed very personal. And very different of course from the previous two. But then, we've been wrong once, could even be wrong twice. I'm being honest – please don't repeat what I've said. So – Just, please, Sir – Dr Merton – be cautious at this time, and urge every-one in the Library, all the Staff and Readers, to be cautious wherever they go, whatever they do, and always to be with other people, never alone. Just in case –

"And we'll be with you soon as possible, then we can talk fur-ther about it. McAllister's just having to deal with a couple important issues first, and then we'll be with you – early afternoon. Kraft won't be able to come – thank goodness."

"Right, we'll be cautious. I'll inform the Staff, and tell them to stay more or less where they are, until you can get here – and I'll send out a telephone and email message immediately. I know you'll inform us exactly about what's happening, and answer our questions, as soon as you can – I'll tell that to the Staff too, and anyone who inquires."

"Good. But there's one more thing, or maybe two things. First, we're going to need to check through the late Librarian's files, so could you –?"

"But that'll take a good while – I mean, for you to read through them. And how far back – to the start of her Librarianship, a few years ago?"

"Oh. Well, just any relating to colleagues – especially the de-ceased Librarian, and the ex-President – Oh, I'll tell you where we're at, why not, I trust you not to tell anyone else. Two possibilities. Mc-Allister thinks it's all connected to that Secret Diary you have in the

Library – he thinks that our Victim the History Professor, who, you remember, was known to have had connections with China, wanted to see the Diary, was desperate to see it, and somebody, maybe the Librarian, was determined that he *wouldn't* see it. Now I don't agree with all that, I think it's far-fetched, but who knows – there's so much that's mysterious about his death, which is why we'll need to interview more people, in fact *everyone* who had any contact at all with the Victim. You included, Sir. Oh, I know you haven't been here long but –"

"And the other possibility?"

"Well, that's *my* theory. The Retirement Scheme that caused so much dissension in the University – you may not know a whole lot about that, but *I* know that it had been causing a whole lot of confusion and bad feelings for quite a while. We have even been told that a lot of that money has disappeared without trace. Which may or may not be true. And we haven't been able to talk yet to your ex-President, who as you may know has apparently suffered a major breakdown after collapsing in his Office. Now, our Victim was a longtime friend and confidant of his, and widely disliked, we've been told, by some of his colleagues – and others in the University community, not only in the History Department –

"Now, here I am, talking too much again. McAllister says I should be called Loose Lips, he likes his little jokes. But I know I can trust you, Sir. And we'll be with you this afternoon and ask you any other questions, and answer *your* questions – so you look after yourself, Sir, and I'm glad you've alerted all your staff just in case –"

Chapter Sixteen

By late morning, Eric was feeling hungry and impatient. He had sent out a warning message, as promised, and tried to calm the increasingly uneasy curiosity around him. He had called Margery again, and Mrs Arthur, and assured them that he was safe of course, and would communicate any information that the Police would, surely, soon provide.

Then, equipped with a small tray of coffee-and-cookies that one of the Staff had generously provided, he decided to go up to his Eyrie for a short break.

Up there, silence. Or near-silence – only the faint hum of distant quiet conversations from below. He dozed.

Until –

"Remember me?"

Eric looked up. "Oh – no. Yes. Didn't we –?"

"Yes, we did. A brief conversation, about this and that. Not very memorable. And, so maybe *you* don't remember, but you *did* invite me to look you up, and the young woman at the Main Desk was able to tell me where you would likely be if you weren't in the Librarian's Office. Looks as if your Retreat is becoming known. Your *Eyrie*, she said you call it. So – here I am." And he smiled. Then continued –

"By the way, do you think *eerie* and *eyrie* were originally the same word? I notice that you do have another chair in your eerie *Eyrie*, haha, so *sit down* again in your chair, Dr Assistant Librarian, and *I'll* sit down here, opposite you. Right.

"So I guess most of the Library Staff and Readers don't even know this exists, your little Retreat, your *Eyrie*. And of course that's why you chose this to be your Retreat, a place for your *eerie* Meditations, hey? So – Ryan, that's my name. Remember now? Ryan."

Eric stood up. "Well – Ryan. I'm glad you've come to visit us. Now I'd better be getting back downstairs to my Office."

"Oh, not just yet, we'll have a friendly chat first." Ryan smiled, then reached into his jacket and drew out a dagger. "So *sit down*."

Eric, shocked, swallowed, sat down.

Silence. Then he rasped "What's this all about? Why are you –?"

"Oh, I'll explain. Briefly – I guess there's not much time. So I'll *need* to be brief, won't I? But it's really quite complicated and of course, you wouldn't know anything much about anything. Just another highly-educated ignoramus, hey! She threatened to tell you, but I didn't take that seriously. Not at first, anyways, she always promised that she wouldn't tell anybody, and as far as I know she never did tell anybody – except of course that swine James Hilton, *Professor* Hilton, and *he* also thought he knew all there was to know about China, because of course *he'd* been there, he said, and we hadn't, *I* hadn't, I'd just read stuff about it – so of course he could sneer at me, at all of us ignorant stupid little Students. 'The greatest Civilization the World has ever known,' that's what he kept on saying, over and over, 'it will soon dominate the whole wide World again, we'll all be at its mercy and *you* ignoramuses don't know *anything* about it' – that's what he was always saying.

"But he thought nobody knew that precious Mary Alderson was his Mistress, even before his wife died, and after she married that rich business-man – And he was good at getting people to tell him *their* secrets, Dr Hilton was, and then he would use what he knew to force people to keep quiet while he – but, well I guess I understood him, mostly he just wanted to make people frightened, *that* gave him a kick, hey? And he totally controlled Mary – used his influence and so that's how she got to be Librarian. *She* was ambitious, and of course *he* knew she was unhappy in her marriage, she was the second wife and the step-daughter hated her. I guess Hilton, the great Dr Hilton, knew *all about her* – and *I* got to know all about *him*.

"Did you know, this is one of my big secrets, I'm only telling you because you won't be able to tell anyone else, but you should have *seen* – But you're not so smart as she thought – She was always raving about *you*, the handsome new Assistant Librarian. And she would say how smart and good-looking you were, and it was like *you* were her son. Same as when I told that Dr Hilton he was my Father, and of course he denied it, said he didn't even know Mary when they were young –

"What a mess they made, those two, *he* ran away from *her* and *she* gave me to those vicious vindictive ignorant *shits* – and the ones who adopted me, they were only in it for the money, those two – I told them that, out loud, and then he beat me up again, and he was always drunk, what a fuckin' loser – But eventually I got help at the School, they were sorry for me, they could see I was being abused, and so then I found out who my real Mother was and so I came here, and she was so shocked, Mary, should have seen her face! – and she must've went straight-away to Dr Hilton, 'It was a mistake, I was young, I was just a girl, and you were older but you were still, like, just a boy, but you gotta help me', something like that – but then she became his Mistress, or maybe that was before – she couldn't deny it, even other people knew about it, even in the Student Res I bet they knew it –

"And then they got me into his Intro Course, Mary and Dr Hilton did – just a Listener, they said, but I bet you I coulda got A-plus. And also *they* got me into the Res – the other kids, all the students in the Res, they all know what's going on – they're not *stupid* –

"So she came here to live near him, but he was married, so he didn't want to know, that's what I think – and so she started working in the Library, and so then he couldn't get away from her and *she* couldn't get away from *him*, Dr James fuckin' Hilton, but she didn't really want to, that's what I think and that's what I told her and she just smiles – and so then he gets more and more control over her when she's the Librarian – he *made* her Librarian, he had Influence in the University – get it? Get it? The great Dr Hilton! He had In-fluence. And she was also his Mistress, did I already say that? Yes, she was. And he knew all about ancient Chinese funeral customs, like painting the corpse's face with red stripes, that's what he said, but then he would say he was only joking, haha – but he didn't care about anybody's feelings, he just sneered at everyone, all us ignorant fuckin' – Dr James bloody Hilton, History Professor – but in the end the Joke was on him, haha.

"But I'm talking too much! *she* would say that – she said I should only talk to *her*, when I want to know things, and she'll always listen and be there for me – And why do you think I killed those two Library guys, her Secretary and then that other one? Because they both hated Mary, and they seen her reading that stupid Secret Diary so they threatened her – she told me that, she was so upset – well, that man, his name was Best but he was Worst, haha, *he* threatened her just because he seen that old Diary on her desk, and Mary says also that the woman that was her Secretary, she had also seen – because Mary was reading it but 'she had no right, it was a crime', that's what stupid Best said to me – 'It's "embargoed"', that's what he said, that Diary, meaning 'it's top secret', and *she* was the one who said that. She told me that, Mary.

"So I just saw him when I went for my run in the Park, I do that nearly every day, and he was sitting on a bench in the shade, near the path, and he says 'Hi' so I stopped, and he says he seen me in the Library, and he tells me he's on the Library Staff, and how he often sees things that aren't right, and that's why he wanted to tell *you*, he's waiting for you, he says, and he says he thinks you are 'trustworthy' haha, you didn't have time yet to learn to be dishonest like the rest, that's what he says. So why's he telling me all this? Maybe he was bored or feeling lonely, like I do sometimes. So he gets more and more friendly, says he's noticed me before in the Library, and I look polite and respectful, haha, not like most students, would I like to have lunch with him, would I like to see where he lives, his apartment – So I sit down on the bench near him and then he says 'When she was the new Librarian, he means Mary, she lectures to us, the whole Staff, about Integrity, and she shows us that Diary, it was in a fancy red box, and she says how nobody, *nobody*, has the right to read it or even open the box until that Embargo come to an end, it's *her* responsibility, it's the Librarian's responsibility.

"And so then he says to me, Best was his name, he seen that box on Mary's desk later, and then also the Secretary has the Diary in front of her and she's reading it! Of course that Best, he didn't know *I* had seen that Diary too, but of course he knows the Secretary is dead now, and so then I see his mouth is open, and he's looking hard at me and I can tell he's starting to be frightened, you can see it in his eyes – and then he jumps up and tries to run away and I stab him in the back – I chase him and stab him in the back –

"But they had no right to threaten Mary, did they, and she was very – she said she might lose her job if I tell anybody. But it was just a accident, with the Secretary– I was looking for Mary, and the Library was closing, I was just leaving, and I was looking for Mary, and that Secretary, she was typing stuff, and looked like it was from that Diary – it was right next to her on the desk, the red box was – and so I just say, like joking, 'And w*hat* are you doing?' and she jumps and gives a little scream and then she picks up the phone but I say 'Put it down' and she – So then I stabbed her and she falls down and then I walk away quickly – And then they say *Mary* did it, the Police, what a fuckin' bloody laugh – and then – and they take Mary away – And so I – And Mary –

"And so, what about *you*? The great Eric Merton, so handsome and ambitious and intelligent – that's what she told me, Mary did – I guess I should call her Mum, hey, but I always just call her Mary, she told me to do that – when I first come here she says that to me – 'Call me Mary like other people do' – but she was so impressed by *you*, 'I really like him', she said that to me – she was always saying that – and then she says 'He's like a son', you're like her son – she says that – '*He's like my son*'. She says that to *me*! *Why* does she say that? To her own son –

"And all that stupid stuff about the famous secret Diary – that's all fuckin' garbage, hey? Who believes all that garbage about a Pandemic – what that old, what's-his-name, Wallace? what he was going on about – that's what she says to me, what his Father wrote in that Diary – he wrote that a Pandemic is coming for the whole wide World – and it will be the beginning of the end of the World, he says –

"No – don't move –"

Eric stood up abruptly, swaying.

He shouted loudly "*Help, help, up here –*"

Ryan lunged at him, stabbed him in the chest, then turned and ran to the stairs.

Eric fell forward, lay bleeding on the floor.